leapfrog

Pus... ...ots

by

Illustrated by Beccy Blake

LONDON • SYDNEY

First published in 2013 by
Franklin Watts
338 Euston Road
London
NW1 3BH

Franklin Watts Australia
Level 17/207 Kent Street
Sydney
NSW 2000

A CIP catalogue record for this book is available
from the British Library.

ISBN 978 1 4451 1615 0 (hbk)
ISBN 978 1 4451 1621 1 (pbk)

Series Editor: Jackie Hamley
Series Advisor: Catherine Glavina
Series Designer: Peter Scoulding

Printed in China

Franklin Watts is a divison of
Hachette Children's Books,
an Hachette UK company.
www.hachette.co.uk

Felix looked at the cat
on the TV.

"I want to be like that cat," Felix thought. "I want to be Puss in Boots."

5

Felix smiled at Princess,
the cat from next door.

Princess washed her face.

Felix turned cartwheels round and round the garden.

One, two, three, four!

He danced along the fence.
"Take that, Buster!"

He made a flying leap
onto the apple tree.

Oh no! Ouch!

Felix saw stars.

He crashed into the

washing pole.

Down came all the clothes.

Felix was trapped!

"Help!" miaowed Felix.

Everyone came running.

Poor Felix.

He was bleeding.

His paws were cut.

His eye looked bad.

Mum called the vet.

20

Felix had to lie on the table. Felix had to say "Aaaah!"

The vet took his temperature. She looked at his cut paws. She gave him a jab.

Felix needed stitches in
both his back paws.
He had to have stitches
in his face.

He was very brave.

"What a soldier," said Dad.

Back at home, Felix saw himself.

"I can't wear a lampshade.
I can't wear boots,"
he miaowed.

"Some cats can wear boots," purred Princess. "Puss in Boots can."

Felix gave her a big smile.

29

Puzzle 1

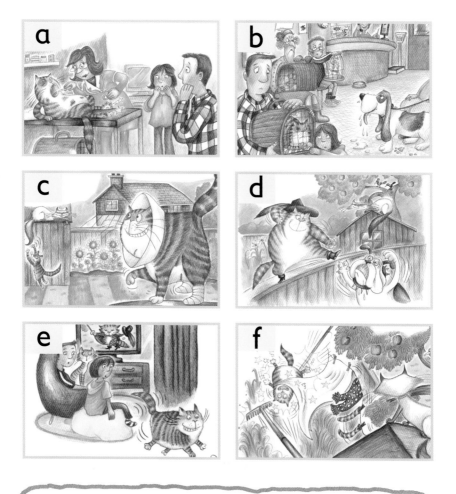

Put these pictures in the correct order.
Now tell the story in your own words.
How short can you make the story?

Puzzle 2

excited   confused

tired

worried   cross

glad

Choose the word which best describes each character. Can you think of any more? Pretend to be one of the characters!

Answers

Puzzle 1

The correct order is:

1e, 2d, 3f, 4b, 5a, 6c

Puzzle 2

Felix The correct word is excited.

The incorrect words are confused, tired.

Dad The correct word is worried.

The incorrect words are cross, glad.

Look out for more Leapfrog stories:

Mary and the Fairy
ISBN 978 0 7496 9142 4

Pippa and Poppa
ISBN 978 0 7496 9140 0

The Bossy Cockerel
ISBN 978 0 7496 9141 7

The Best Snowman
ISBN 978 0 7496 9143 1

Big Bad Blob
ISBN 978 0 7496 7796 1

Cara's Breakfast
ISBN 978 0 7496 7797 8

Sticky Vickie
ISBN 978 0 7496 7986 6

Handyman Doug
ISBN 978 0 7496 7987 3

The Wrong House
ISBN 978 0 7496 9480 7

Prickly Ballroom
ISBN 978 0 7496 9475 3

That Noise!
ISBN 978 0 7496 9479 1

The Scary Chef's Scarecrow
ISBN 978 0 7496 9476 0

Alex and the Troll
ISBN 978 0 7496 9478 4

The Frog Prince and the Kitten
ISBN 978 1 4451 1614 3*
ISBN 978 1 4451 1620 4

The Animals' Football Cup
ISBN 978 0 7496 9477 7

The Animals' Football Camp
ISBN 978 1 4451 1610 5*
ISBN 978 1 4451 1616 7

Bill's Bouncy Shoes
ISBN 978 0 7496 7990 3

Bill's Scary Backpack
ISBN 978 0 7496 9468 5

Bill's Silly Hat
ISBN 978 1 4451 1611 2*
ISBN 978 1 4451 1617 4

Little Joe's Balloon Race
ISBN 978 0 7496 7989 7

Little Joe's Boat Race
ISBN 978 0 7496 9467 8

Little Joe's Horse Race
ISBN 978 1 4451 1613 6*
ISBN 978 1 4451 1619 8

Felix and the Kitten
ISBN 978 0 7496 7988 0

Felix Takes the Blame
ISBN 978 0 7496 9466 1

Felix, Puss in Boots
ISBN 978 1 4451 1615 0*
ISBN 978 1 4451 1621 1

Cheeky Monkey on Holiday
ISBN 978 0 7496 7991 0

Cheeky Monkey's Treasure Hunt
ISBN 978 0 7496 9465 4

Cheeky Monkey's Big Race
ISBN 978 1 4451 1612 9*
ISBN 978 1 4451 1618 1

For details of all our titles go to: www.franklinwatts.co.uk

*hardback